A Treasury of
Christmas
Stories and
Songs

This edition published by Parragon Books Ltd in 2014

Parragon Books Ltd
Chartist House
15–17 Trim Street
Bath BA1 1HA, UK
www.parragon.com

Edited by Catherine Ard and Michael Diggle
Designed by Kathryn Davies
Production by Marina Blackburn

ISBN 978-1-4723-7551-3

Printed in China

A Treasury of Christmas Stories and Songs

Arthur
Christmas
2015
♡ Uncle Dean
Auntie
Liz & Henry
Luzie &
Edward
xx

PaRragon

Bath • New York • Cologne • Melbourne • Delhi
Hong Kong • Shenzhen • Singapore • Amsterdam

Contents

The First Christmas

Long ago in a place called Nazareth there lived a girl called Mary. She was engaged to be married to a carpenter called Joseph, and she would daydream about their wedding as she went about her chores.

One day, as she swept the yard, Mary noticed a stranger smiling at her. She knew at once that he was an angel.

"My name is Gabriel," he said. "I have brought you a message from God."

Mary was too amazed to speak.

"God has chosen you to do something special for him," continued Gabriel. "Soon, you will have a baby, and you are to call him Jesus. He will be God's own son."

Mary was happy to do as God had asked, but Joseph felt upset because he knew he wasn't the father of the baby. He prayed to God for help.

"What should I do?" he asked. "I love Mary, but I don't know if I should still marry her."

God heard his prayers. That night, an angel visited Joseph in a dream.

"Do not worry," he told Joseph. "This baby will become a king and save his people."

"I will trust in God," Joseph decided the next morning.

So Mary and Joseph were married and they
waited patiently for the baby to arrive.

Soon after the wedding, the Emperor of Rome, who ruled over the land where Mary and Joseph lived, sent out orders through his messengers.

"Everyone must travel to their place of birth to be counted," said the messengers.

Joseph had been born in Bethlehem, a long way away.

"My wife is going to have a baby soon," said Joseph.

"Can we go to Bethlehem another time?"

The messenger shook his head. "Everyone must go now," he said.

Joseph packed enough food and water for the
journey, and Mary made a bundle of blankets and clothes
for when the baby arrived. They said their goodbyes to
friends and family and set out for Bethlehem.

The journey to Bethlehem took
many days. The roads were dusty and
the sun shone brightly.

It was late at night when they
finally arrived, and Mary was very tired.

"Let's find a place to stay for the
night," said Joseph. But every inn they
tried was full.

16

When they arrived at the last inn in town, the owner shook his head.

"There is no room at the inn," he said. "Everyone has come to Bethlehem to obey the Emperor's order."

"What can we do?" asked Mary. "My baby is coming very soon."

"Come," said the man kindly. "I have a place that might do."

The innkeeper led them to a stable behind the house. It was filled with animals and the floor was covered with fresh straw.

"This is warm and safe," said Mary. "Thank you for your kindness."

That night, Mary gave birth to a little boy.

Joseph lined a feeding trough with
straw to make a soft bed. Mary wrapped
the baby in a blanket and laid him down
gently in the manger.

"We'll call you Jesus, like the angel
said," whispered Mary.

Nearby, some shepherds were watching over their sheep on a hillside.

Suddenly there was a dazzling brightness all around them.

"What's happening?" they cried, as an angel appeared.

"Don't be afraid," said the angel. "I have wonderful news. The son of God has been born in Bethlehem. He is the king that God promised."

The light faded and the angel was gone.
The shepherds looked at each other in wonder.
"We must go to Bethlehem and see the
baby king," they agreed.

The shepherds walked
through the quiet streets until
they heard a baby's cry and
found the stable.

"We have come to visit the
new king," they said. "God sent
an angel to give us the news."

"You are all welcome,"
said Joseph.

"We are poor," said the shepherds as they knelt by the manger. "We have nothing to give the baby but our love."

"That is the best gift in the world," said Mary.

Soon it was time for the shepherds to return to their sheep. They told everyone they met about the new king.

In a far-off country, three wise men noticed a new star
in the sky. They knew that this meant something special.

"It is shining because a new king has been born," said one.

"Perhaps the star will lead us to him," said the second.

"Let's take some gifts and go and worship this king," said the third.

The wise men set off for the city of Jerusalem. They were sure they would find the new king there, at the palace.

After travelling for many nights,
the wise men arrived at the palace. They
were taken to the ruler, King Herod.

"We have come to worship the new
king," they said.

King Herod was worried. He wanted
to be the only king in the land.

"Who is this new king they speak
of?" he whispered to his advisor.

"A prophet once said that a new
king would be born in Bethlehem,"
the advisor said.

King Herod decided he must stop the baby taking his throne.
"I want to worship the new king too," he lied. "Go to Bethlehem,
then return here and tell me where I can find him."

The wise men travelled to Bethlehem,
where the star led them to the stable.

"We have come to see the new king,"
said the wise men.

Mary welcomed them in and they
knelt to give Jesus their gifts.

"Here is precious gold," said the first.

"I have brought sweet-smelling
frankincense," said the second.

"And this is myrrh, a healing oil,"
said the third.

That night the wise men camped
outside Bethlehem.
While they slept, God visited
each of them in a dream. He warned
them not to return to King Herod.
In the morning, the wise men
agreed to go straight home.

King Herod was furious when he learned
that the wise men had disobeyed him.
"I am the only king!" he roared.
"I will not let a baby take my throne!"

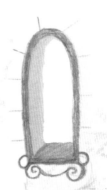

God sent an angel to warn Joseph that Herod was planning to harm Jesus.

"You must leave Bethlehem at once," said the angel. "Escape to Egypt, where you will be safe."

Joseph woke Mary and they quickly loaded their belongings onto the donkey. Carrying Jesus, they set off into the night.

Jesus was safe in Egypt, but Mary and Joseph missed Nazareth.

A few years passed peacefully. One night, God sent an angel to speak to Joseph in a dream.

"King Herod has died," said the angel. "It is safe for you to return home."

Joseph and Mary packed their belongings and set off once more. When they arrived, they were overjoyed to be back in their hometown at last.

Joseph held Jesus as he stood in the doorway of their little house.
"This is Nazareth, the town where you will grow up," he said
with a smile. "Welcome home, Jesus!"

Hark! The Herald Angels Sing

Hark! The herald angels sing,
"Glory to the new-born king."
Peace on earth and mercy mild,
God and sinners reconciled.
Joyful, all you nations rise,
Join the triumph of the skies.
With the angelic hosts proclaim,
"Christ is born in Bethlehem."
Hark! The herald angels sing,
"Glory to the new-born king."

O Christmas Tree

O Christmas Tree, O Christmas Tree,
How lovely are your branches!
Not only green when summer's here,
But in the coldest time of year.
O Christmas Tree, O Christmas Tree,
How lovely are your branches!

The Nutcracker

It was Christmas Eve and the snow was gently falling. Clara and her brother Fritz were very excited. That night there would be a magnificent party with music and dancing, as well as lots of fantastic presents!

Fritz was busy with his toy soldiers, lining them up and giving them their orders.

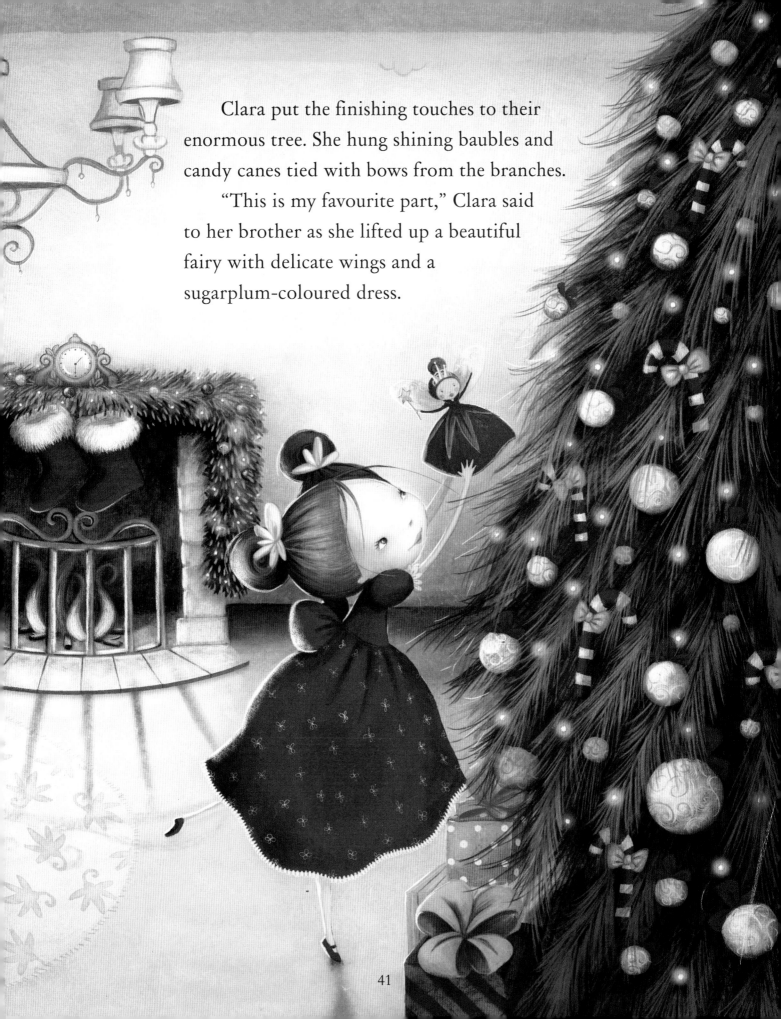

Clara put the finishing touches to their enormous tree. She hung shining baubles and candy canes tied with bows from the branches.

"This is my favourite part," Clara said to her brother as she lifted up a beautiful fairy with delicate wings and a sugarplum-coloured dress.

At last, it was time for
the party to begin.

"The guests are arriving!"
cried Clara, peeping out of her
bedroom window.

Fritz came running over to see
who was crunching through the snow.

"Can you see Godfather
Drosselmeyer?" asked Clara.

"Yes, there he is waving!"
cried Fritz. "Come on!"

Their godfather was a famous
toymaker. He made the most magical
toys in the whole city. Clara and Fritz
could hardly wait to see what he had
brought for them.

Godfather Drosselmeyer hugged the
children at the door, and with a flourish,
he produced two gifts.

Fritz eagerly unwrapped a mechanical
gobstopper machine. For Clara, there was a
wooden nutcracker in the shape of a soldier.

"Take good care of him," said Godfather
Drosselmeyer. "He is very special."

"I love him," Clara whispered.
"Thank you."

"But he's a soldier," said Fritz. "He should be mine."

"You can't have him!" cried Clara.

Fritz tried to snatch the Nutcracker away from her. He pulled and Clara tugged, and then...

CRACK!

The Nutcracker's leg snapped off!

Clara cradled the Nutcracker in her arms and wept.

"Don't cry, Clara," said her godfather gently. "This soldier has been wounded, but I can soon fix him."

Godfather Drosselmeyer pulled a little tool pouch from his pocket and quickly mended the Nutcracker so that he looked as good as new.

"Oh, thank you," said Clara, drying her eyes. "I'll never let anyone hurt him again."

Everyone was dancing now and the house was filled with music and laughter. Clara placed the Nutcracker carefully under the Christmas tree and went to join the party.

Finally, the last dance was danced and the guests said their goodbyes. The family went to bed and the house was dark and quiet.

Bong!

Clara awoke to hear the last bong of the clock striking midnight.
"Oh no!" she thought. "I left the Nutcracker all alone under the tree."
Clara tiptoed downstairs and crept under the Christmas tree, holding the Nutcracker protectively.

Suddenly, the tree started to
grow. Taller and taller! Or was it
just that Clara was shrinking?
    "What's happening?" she cried.

"Don't be afraid," said a kind voice suddenly.
Clara turned around. Her Nutcracker had come alive!
Behind him, Fritz's soldiers were sitting up in their
toy box and Clara's dolls were gazing around.

Before Clara could speak, she heard a scurrying
sound and from every nook and cranny, an army of
mice poured into the room! They were led by
a giant Mouse King with a golden crown.

"ATTACK!" he squealed.

"Who will fight with me?" cried the Nutcracker.
The soldiers marched boldly out of the toy box.

"TO BATTLE!" ordered the Nutcracker.
The soldiers shouted and cheered and the
mice squealed and squeaked.

Suddenly, Clara saw the Mouse King spring towards her beloved Nutcracker, baring his teeth.

"No!" cried Clara. She snatched off her slipper and hurled it at the Mouse King. He fell to the ground with a cry, and his crown tumbled from his head.

With their leader defeated, the mice scurried away in fear. The battle was won!

The Nutcracker picked up Clara's
slipper and placed it on her foot. She
gasped – the Nutcracker had been
transformed into a handsome prince!

"I owe you my life, Princess Clara," he said.
"You broke the spell that was put on me long
ago by a wicked Mouse Queen."

"I'm glad that you're safe," said Clara.
"But you are mistaken – I'm not a princess."

"Are you sure?" asked the prince.

Clara looked down and saw that she was
wearing a glittering gown and satin shoes!

"Come," said the prince. "I am going to
take you on a wonderful adventure."

The walls of the sitting room seemed to fade away, and a beautiful sleigh drew up in front of them, led by two reindeer.

Clara and the prince climbed aboard and they were swept high into the sky among the sparkling stars.

Suddenly Clara caught sight of a magical land down below. Lollipop trees shimmered on candyfloss hills. There were gingerbread houses and rivers of honey, and an orange-scented breeze.

"Where are we?" gasped Clara.

"This is the Kingdom of Sweets," said the prince.

The sleigh landed beside a rose-coloured lake and changed into a sea-chariot pulled by dolphins. Swans swam beside them, and shimmering fish leapt out of the water.

On the far side of the lake was a magnificent marzipan palace. A fairy with delicate wings was waving to them from the gate.

"Look," said the prince. "It's the Sugarplum Fairy!"

"Prince Nutcracker!" cried the fairy. "You are home at last."

"This is Princess Clara," said the prince, as they stepped ashore. "She saved my life and broke the Mouse Queen's spell."

The Sugarplum Fairy hugged Clara.

"Come and join the celebrations!" she said.

Inside the palace, Clara and the prince
feasted on delicious cakes and sweets.

They watched in wonder as dancers
from every corner of the world whirled
around the room.

Then it was the Sugarplum Fairy's turn. Clara had never seen such dancing! She twirled and twirled until all Clara could see was the blur of her plum-coloured dress.

Clara's eyelids began to droop. Her adventures had made her tired. The sound of the music became fainter and fainter....

When Clara woke up on Christmas morning, she found herself curled up under the Christmas tree next to the Nutcracker. Toys were strewn across the floor and her parents were standing over her.

"What have you been doing?" asked her father.

"Oh, I've had the most wonderful adventure," said Clara.

She told her parents all about the Mouse King, the Nutcracker Prince and the Kingdom of Sweets.

"It was just a dream, darling," said her mother.

Clara gazed up at the sugarplum-coloured fairy on top of the tree. Then she looked at the wooden Nutcracker in her hands.

"Perhaps it was," she said.

Suddenly, Clara noticed something glinting on the carpet and a smile spread across her face. It was a tiny golden crown!

"Merry Christmas, Prince
Nutcracker," she whispered.

Away in a Manger

Away in a manger, no crib for a bed,
The little Lord Jesus laid down His sweet head.
The stars in the bright sky looked down where He lay,
The little Lord Jesus asleep on the hay.

The cattle are lowing, the baby awakes,
But Little Lord Jesus, no crying he makes.
I love Thee, Lord Jesus; look down from the sky,
And stay by my side until morning is nigh.

Be near me, Lord Jesus, I ask Thee to stay
Close by me forever, and love me, I pray.
Bless all the dear children in Thy tender care,
And fit us for heaven, to live with Thee there.

We Wish You a Merry Christmas

We wish you a Merry Christmas,
We wish you a Merry Christmas,
We wish you a Merry Christmas,
And a Happy New Year!

Good tidings we bring
To you and your kin;
We wish you a Merry Christmas,
And a Happy New Year!

The Snow Queen

Once, there was a wicked imp who made a magic mirror. Everything it reflected looked ugly and mean. The most beautiful princess would look dreadful. The sunniest day would seem rainy and cold.

One day, some careless sprites took the mirror, but it fell from their hands. It smashed into tiny specks, each no bigger than a grain of sand. The glass specks got into people's eyes and made everything look bad to them. Some specks became caught in people's hearts, making them feel cross and grumpy.

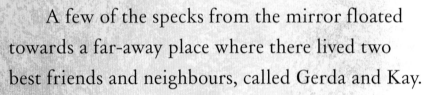

A few of the specks from the mirror floated towards a far-away place where there lived two best friends and neighbours, called Gerda and Kay.

The pair spent endless days together. In the winter, Gerda's grandmother told them wonderful stories while the snow swirled outside.

"The Snow Queen brings the winter weather," she would say. "She peeps in at the windows and leaves icy patterns on the glass."

In the summer, the children would play in the little roof garden between their houses. One sunny day, they were reading together when Kay let out a cry.

"Ouch! I felt a pain in my chest, and now there is something in my eye!" he exclaimed. Specks from the imp's magic mirror had caught in Kay's eye and his heart.

"These roses stink," he said with a frown.

Gerda couldn't understand why Kay was suddenly so cross.

Kay was bad-tempered throughout the summer and the autumn and was still cross when winter came. One snowy day, Kay stormed off with his sledge, looking for ways he could cause some mischief.

Suddenly, a large white sleigh swept past and Kay quickly hitched his sledge to the back.

With a swoosh, Kay was off! The sleigh pulled him through the streets, faster and faster – out of the town and into the countryside.

When the sleigh finally stopped, a majestic figure turned slowly towards Kay. He couldn't believe his eyes – it was the Snow Queen from Gerda's grandmother's story! The queen kissed Kay's forehead and her icy touch froze Kay's heart. He forgot all about Gerda and his home.

Gerda missed Kay. She searched all through the town and
then down by the river, but Kay wasn't there. Just as she was
about to give up, Gerda noticed a little boat among the rushes.

"Perhaps the river will carry me to Kay," she thought.
She climbed in and the boat glided away.

Gerda floated along for many hours, until at last, the boat reached the shore.

A large raven came hopping towards her.

"Hello," he croaked. "Where are you going, little girl?"

Gerda was amazed to hear the raven speak, but he seemed kind, so she told him about Kay.

"I think I have seen your friend," the raven said. "A young man that sounds like him has married a princess close by. My sister lives at the palace. She could take you to him."

That night, the raven's sister led Gerda
up a narrow staircase to the palace bedroom
where the prince and princess slept.
Gerda lifted her lamp.
"Kay!" she called excitedly. "It's me, Gerda!"
The prince opened his eyes and gazed at
her in surprise – but he wasn't Kay.

Poor Gerda! She was hungry and far from home.
She told the prince and princess her story,
and the princess hugged her.

"Let us help you," she said. "Sleep here
tonight and tomorrow you can continue your
journey in comfort."

The next morning, Gerda was given warm clothes and a golden sleigh. She set off into the woods, but before long she was spotted by a band of robbers.

"That carriage is pure gold!" they hissed.

The robbers sprang out and captured Gerda, ready to take her away to their castle.

Suddenly the daughter of the robber chief appeared. Her hair was tangled and her eyes were black as coal. The girl was lonely and excited by the thought of a new friend.

"Please, treat her gently!" the robber girl pleaded. "She can stay with me."

The robbers' castle was guarded by
mean-looking bulldogs. Magpies and rooks
squawked from the crumbling battlements.
Gerda was grateful to the robber girl
for her kindness. She would have been very
scared if she'd been all alone.

Inside, Gerda met the robber girl's pigeons and
her pet reindeer. Gerda told her new friend about Kay.

That night, as the girls slept, the pigeons began to coo.

"Gerda, we have seen Kay," said the pigeons. "He was
travelling to Lapland with the Snow Queen, under her spell."

Gerda sat up, feeling hopeful again.

"I know the way to the Snow Queen's palace," added
the reindeer.

Gerda woke the robber girl and told her what the animals
had said. The robber girl quickly untied the reindeer.

"Take Gerda to Lapland," she said. "She must
find her friend."

It was a long, cold journey, but at last Gerda and the
reindeer arrived in Lapland. They stopped at a crooked little
cottage. The wise old woman who lived there knew all about Kay.

"Can you help Gerda defeat the Snow Queen?" the reindeer
quietly asked the wise woman, as Gerda sat by the fire.

The wise woman shook her head. "Gerda doesn't need my help,"
she whispered. "Her love for her friend is strong enough."

The next morning, the reindeer
carried Gerda to the edge of the
Snow Queen's garden. He set her
down and she started to run through
the snow towards the palace.

Inside the ice palace, the beautiful Snow Queen still held Kay under her spell.

As she sat on her throne, the Snow Queen watched as Kay struggled to fit together some pieces of ice.

"You can go free when you have completed my puzzle," the Snow Queen told him. "All you have to do is spell out the word 'Eternity'."

No matter how many times he tried to solve
the puzzle, Kay could not spell out the word.

"Spring is coming," said the Snow Queen, suddenly, and she rose from her throne in a great hurry. "It is time for me to make it snow on the other side of the world!"

She flew off in her sleigh, leaving Kay alone.

At that moment, Gerda crept into the palace.

"Kay!" Gerda cried. She ran to her friend and hugged him. Her tears fell onto his chest. They melted his cold heart and washed away the speck of glass. Kay began to cry too, and his tears washed the glass from his eye.

"Gerda!" Kay shouted in excitement.

The children's joy made the puzzle pieces dance among the spikes of ice. When the pieces settled again, they spelt out the word 'Eternity', freeing Kay from the Snow Queen's spell.

The reindeer carried Gerda and Kay away from the
palace to the edge of Lapland, where the snow disappeared.
"This is the start of spring," said the reindeer. "And
now I must say goodbye."
"Goodbye, and thank you!" said Gerda and Kay.

As the reindeer left, someone rode out of the trees on a
beautiful horse and waved to them. It was the robber girl.

Gerda went to meet her and they hugged each other happily.

"I am glad that you found Kay," she said. "I must go now,
but one day I will visit you."

Gerda and Kay walked for days on end. The spring flowers bloomed and blossomed, and when at last they heard the church bells ringing, they knew they were close to home.

"Grandmother!" called Gerda. "We're back at last!"

She ran up the stairs with Kay and found her grandmother sitting in the sunshine, reading her book. The old lady wrapped them in her arms and hugged them tightly.

"I knew that you would come home one day," she said.

They sat together in the little roof garden and told Gerda's grandmother all about their adventures.

95

Each year the Snow Queen brought the winter weather. And each year, when the snow swirled outside, Kay and Gerda stayed safe and warm inside, listening to Gerda's grandmother's wonderful stories.

Jingle Bells

Dashing through the snow,
In a one-horse open sleigh,
O'er the fields we go,
Laughing all the way.
Bells on bob-tail ring,
Making spirits bright,
What fun it is to laugh and sing
A sleighing song tonight!

Oh! Jingle bells! Jingle bells!
Jingle all the way!
Oh, what fun it is to ride
In a one-horse open sleigh!
Jingle bells! Jingle bells!
Jingle all the way!
Oh, what fun it is to ride
In a one-horse open sleigh!

Deck the Halls

Deck the halls with boughs of holly,

Fa la la la la, la la la la.

'Tis the season to be jolly,

Fa la la la la, la la la la.

Don we now our gay apparel,

Fa la la, la la la, la la la.

Troll the ancient Yuletide carol,

Fa la la la la, la la la la.

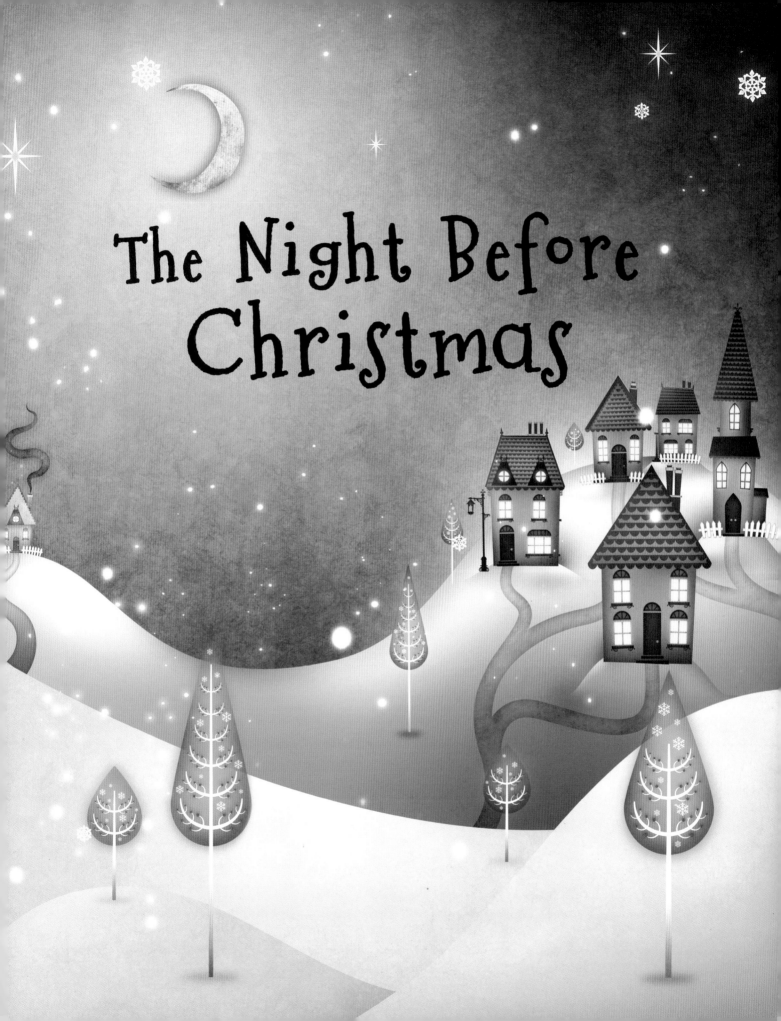

The Night Before Christmas

'Twas the night before Christmas,
when all through the house
Not a creature was stirring,
not even a mouse.

The stockings were hung
by the chimney with care,
In hope that St Nicholas
soon would be there.

The children were nestled all snug in their beds,
While visions of sugarplums danced in their heads.

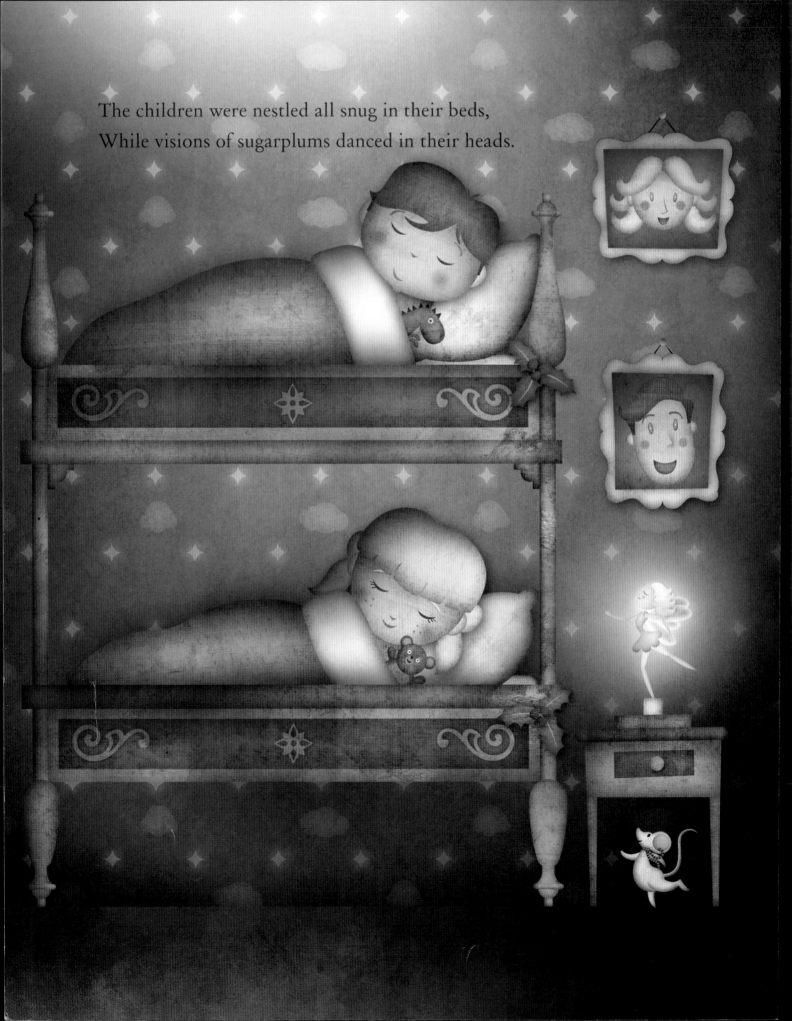

And Mama in her 'kerchief and I in my cap,
Had just settled down for a long winter's nap.
When out on the lawn there arose such a clatter,
I sprang from my bed to see what was the matter.

Away to the window I flew like a flash,
Tore open the shutters and threw up the sash.
The moon on the breast of the new-fallen snow
Gave lustre of midday to objects below,
When, what to my wondering eyes should appear,
But a miniature sleigh and eight tiny reindeer.

With a little old driver so lively and quick,
I knew in a moment it must be St Nick.

More rapid than eagles
his coursers they came,
And he whistled and shouted
and called them by name;

"Now Dasher! Now Dancer! Now Prancer and Vixen!
On Comet! On Cupid! On Donner and Blitzen!

112

"To the top of the porch! To the top of the wall!
Now dash away! Dash away! Dash away all!"

113

As dry leaves that before the wild hurricane fly,
When they meet with an obstacle, mount to the sky,
So up to the housetop the coursers they flew,

With a sleigh full of toys and St Nicholas, too.
And then in a twinkling, I heard on the roof
The prancing and pawing of each little hoof.

As I drew in my head and was turning around,
Down the chimney St Nicholas came with a bound.

He was dressed all in fur, from his head to his foot,
And his clothes were all tarnished with ashes and soot.
A bundle of toys he had flung on his back,
And he looked like a pedlar just opening his pack.

His eyes – how they twinkled!
His dimples – how merry!
His cheeks were like roses, his nose like a cherry!
His droll little mouth was drawn up like a bow,
And the beard of his chin was as white as the snow.

He had a broad face and a little round belly,
That shook when he laughed, like a bowlful of jelly.

He was chubby and plump, a right jolly old elf,
And I laughed when I saw him, in spite of myself.
A wink of his eye and a twist of his head,
Soon gave me to know I had nothing to dread.

He spoke not a word but went straight to his work,
And filled all the stockings, then turned with a jerk,

And laying his finger aside of his nose
And giving a nod, up the chimney he rose.

126

He sprang to his sleigh, to his team gave a whistle,
And away they all flew like the down of a thistle.
But I heard him exclaim ere he drove out of sight,
"Merry Christmas to all, and to all a goodnight!"

The First Noel

The first Noel, the angels did say
Was to certain poor shepherds in fields as they lay;
In fields where they lay, keeping their sheep,
On a cold winter's night that was so deep.

Noel, Noel, Noel, Noel
Born is the King of Israel.

Good King Wenceslas

Good King Wenceslas looked out, on the Feast of Stephen,
When the snow lay round about, deep and crisp and even;
Brightly shone the moon that night, tho' the frost was cruel,
When a poor man came in sight, gath'ring winter fuel.

A Letter to Santa

To Santa,
Santa's Grotto,
North Pole

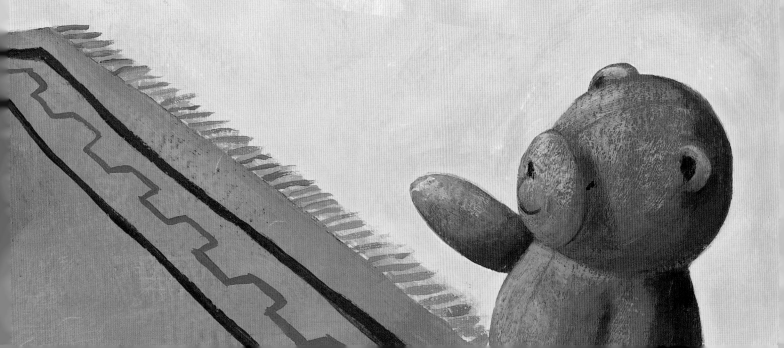

On Christmas Eve, when the snow was all white,
I sat on the floor with a letter to write.
Before I began, I thought what to say
I'd like Santa to leave for me on Christmas Day.

Dear Santa,
(I neatly wrote)
I hope you are well
when you read this note.
I'm sure you have noticed
that I have been good,
just as my mummy
told me I should.
So if it's alright,
for Christmas I'd like —
a book or a train set
or maybe a bike.

Then when I'd finished, I printed my name,
And added kisses again and again.

Across to the fireplace I boldly went,
And up the chimney my letter was sent.
For that is the place, I'm sure you will know,
That letters to Santa should always go.
Just how they get there, I don't understand,
But that is the way to Santa's cold land.

That winter's night when the world was asleep,
I snuggled in bed – not a sound, not a peep –
Thinking of Santa and the toys he would bring,
And the fun I would have on Christmas morning.
When, all of a sudden, where could I be?
Out in the snow in a strange country!

Next to a cabin in the deep crispy snow,
I shiver with cold as I peer in the window.
It's Santa's workshop! I must creep inside.
No one will see me if I'm careful to hide.
Sssh! I must be quiet as I tiptoe in,
To see where our Christmas toys all begin.

Santa's Grotto

I can see Santa reading letters galore.
Hey, he's got mine, by his feet on the floor!
A map of the world is pinned to the wall,
Showing Santa the way to the homes of us all,
With rooftop instructions so there is no doubt,
That any small child is ever left out.

Just see how busy all Santa's elves are:
One's making a doll's house, one a toy car;
Another elf's painting a wonderful train,

And this elf is putting the wings on a plane.
Look at that little elf riding a bike,
It's just like the one I said I would like.

This must be the room where presents are packed.
They're measured for size, then carefully wrapped.
Tied up with ribbons and finished with bows,
Each with a name tag so Santa Claus knows.
Wherever you look there's bustle and scurry.
Everyone seems in a terrible hurry.

Here are the elves who help Santa get dressed.
There's Santa's coat and hat, all neatly pressed.
And there are his boots getting a shine.
They look so smart, I wish they were mine!
I think this room is as good as the rest,
For it's the place that makes Santa look best.

Back in the workshop, the parcel track halts.
It seems there's a problem with one of its bolts!
The elves are worried – there's trouble in the air.
But here comes Santa to make the repair.
In no time at all, parcels speed on their way,
Out to the stables and onto the sleigh.

Outside the stable, the reindeer wait.
I count them all up, and yes, there are eight!
Their hooves are polished, their bells burnished bright,
As elves brush and groom them in the moonlight.
Their harnesses gleam, their coats all shine.
Now the reindeer are restless, as it's almost time!

The sleigh is now packed and the reindeer ready.
Santa at the reins cries, "Away now, go steady!"
High over clouds and hills they fly,
Galloping onwards across the sky.
Soon, beneath them, rooftops they see
Where inside asleep are children like me!

When I wake up, it's Christmas Day,
And just like my dream, Santa's been! Hooray!
My stocking is filled up with candy canes,
And I'm sure in that parcel there must be a train.
Great! There's a bicycle propped by my bed.
My letter to Santa must have been read!

We Three Kings

We three Kings of Orient are,
Bearing gifts we travel afar,
Field and fountain, moor and mountain,
Following yonder star.

O star of wonder, star of night,
Star with royal beauty bright,
Westward leading, still proceeding,
Guide us to thy perfect light.

O Little Town of Bethlehem

O little town of Bethlehem
How still we see thee lie.
Above thy deep and dreamless sleep
The silent stars go by.
Yet in thy dark streets shineth
The everlasting light.
The hopes and fears of all the years
Are met in thee tonight.

On the first day of Christmas
my true love sent to me
A partridge in a pear tree.

On the second day of Christmas
   my true love sent to me
Two turtle doves

And a partridge in a pear tree.

On the third day of Christmas
my true love sent to me
Three French hens,

Two turtle doves
And a partridge in a pear tree.

On the fourth day of Christmas
my true love sent to me
Four calling birds,

Three French hens,
Two turtle doves
And a partridge in a pear tree.

On the fifth day of Christmas
my true love sent to me

Five golden rings...

Four calling birds,
Three French hens,
Two turtle doves
And a partridge in a pear tree.

On the sixth day of Christmas
my true love sent to me
Six geese a-laying,

Five golden rings,
Four calling birds,
Three French hens,
Two turtle doves
And a partridge in a pear tree.

On the seventh day of Christmas
my true love sent to me
Seven swans a-swimming,

Six geese a-laying,
Five golden rings,
Four calling birds,
Three French hens,
Two turtle doves
And a partridge in a pear tree.

On the eighth day of Christmas
  my true love sent to me
Eight maids a-milking,

Seven swans a-swimming,
Six geese a-laying,
Five golden rings,
Four calling birds,
Three French hens,
Two turtle doves
And a partridge in a pear tree.

On the ninth day of Christmas
my true love sent to me
Nine ladies dancing,

Eight maids a-milking,
Seven swans a-swimming,
Six geese a-laying,
Five golden rings,
Four calling birds,
Three French hens,
Two turtle doves
And a partridge in a pear tree.

On the tenth day of Christmas
my true love sent to me
Ten lords a-leaping,

Nine ladies dancing,
Eight maids a-milking,
Seven swans a-swimming,
Six geese a-laying,
Five golden rings,
Four calling birds,
Three French hens,
Two turtle doves
And a partridge in a pear tree.

On the eleventh day of Christmas
my true love sent to me
Eleven pipers piping,

Ten lords a-leaping,
Nine ladies dancing,
Eight maids a-milking,
Seven swans a-swimming,
Six geese a-laying,
Five golden rings,
Four calling birds,
Three French hens,
Two turtle doves
And a partridge in a pear tree.

On the twelfth day of Christmas
my true love sent to me
Twelve drummers drumming,

Eleven pipers piping,
Ten lords a-leaping,
Nine ladies dancing,
Eight maids a-milking,
Seven swans a-swimming,
Six geese a-laying,
Five golden rings,
Four calling birds,
Three French hens,
Two turtle doves
And a partridge in a pear tree!

Silent Night

Silent night, holy night,
All is calm, all is bright;
Round yon virgin mother and child,
Holy infant so tender and mild,
Sleep in heavenly peace,
Sleep in heavenly peace.

O Come, All Ye Faithful

O come, all ye faithful,
Joyful and triumphant!
O come ye, O come ye to Bethlehem;

Come and behold him,
Born the King of Angels;
O come, let us adore Him,
O come, let us adore Him,
O come, let us adore Him,
Christ the Lord.